The Adventures of Colin the Dog

GW00760010

Special thanks to Kate Chesterton for the illustration. She's done some amazing work all over the place but in particular on the books Finding Happiness and Looking for Love that I strongly recommend.

Also, thanks to Jo for creative input and Hazel for invaluable editing work.

Contents

1. The Day of the Blizzard

In the spring of 1966
came gales that roared and rattled the bricks.
The hills of Sheffield crouched and hid
from the rain that crashed and smashed and hit.

People went scurrying around the town
with collars turned up to the rain coming down.
Brollies long gone in the terrible wind;
the rattle and clatter of wind battered bins.

A young, single mum was braving the lot;
she was pushing a pram with her teeny wee tot.
She had to get med's for the littl'un you see
but she was scared and wind-beaten and cold as can be.

At the top of the hill, looking down to the shops,
she braces herself and she can't help but stop
when a huge gust of wind knocks her head over feet
and she falls to the floor in a withering heap.

But the pram, oh the pram, that's the worst thing you know,
as the poor lady fell, well of course she let go!
The pram started slowly to roll down the hill

but with wind it went faster, with slope faster still.

The mum cried in vain in the hurricane winds

but the pram went on rolling as the rain spattered in.

It was flying towards - oh, it's too bad to say!

A huge, busy road with traffic both ways.

Oh no, what to do? This ending looks dark.

But wait just a minute, did I hear a bark?

The mother looked on with her hands in the air

when a dog whipped right by her, with pretty grey hair.

He wore a bandana of rich ruby red,

had a shock of white hair on the top of his head.

"It's Colin" she cried! "But what can he do?

My pram's going faster than horses from glue".

But Colin's quite special and my how he moved,

he shot down the hill as the wind 'n' rain blew.

He caught up with the pram and grabbed onto the rack

with his little grey jaw, then he arched up his back.

He pushed down with his paws but the road had no give,

he pulled and he pulled and along Colin slid.

The pram slowed at last and with no room to spare

the baby was saved! Dog had answered the prayer.

The mother came running with tears on her face,
she grabbed up her baby and what an embrace;
then she turned to see Colin limping away
with blood covered paw prints and coat shiny grey.

She ran after Colin and said "thank you so much,
I'll thank you forever, you were sent from above".
Of course Colin's a dog and he cannot talk
and because of the bleeding he struggles to walk;
but if Colin could talk I know what he'd say
"I saved a life on a cold winter's day,
it's an honour I think to help boys and girls
And as I saved a life there's more love in the world".

So off wandered Colin, his tail in the air,
his ruby red neckerchief, his fluffy grey hair,
his heart a bit fuller as he'd done a good thing,
"I'm glad I'm a wonder dog, but my paws sure do sting".

2. The Day the Dog Saved

There once was a dog named Colin
with a grey beard and a fluffy grey tail.
He wore a fine scarlet bandana
which he'd clean every day without fail.

He loved chasing squirrels in the forest,
he loved to run pell-mell through leaves,
he'd roll around in big muddy puddles
and sometimes he'd even climb trees
('though he wasn't very good at that on account of his stumpy legs).

But one day he walked out of the forest
and saw a small child in the street
with a car flying directly toward him
and the silly child dragging his feet!

So Colin went flying his tail in the air,
he leapt and he dived he had no time to spare,
he flew like the wind at the chest of the kid
who was flung out the way as the car did a skid.

Onlookers screamed and they heard the dog yelp;
at the side of the road the frightened boy knelt.
"That dog saved your life" the driver then simpered,
"but where is the dog?" the little boy whimpered.

The crowd stood and stared looking frightfully shocked
while nervous and crying the little boy rocked,
he thought "that's the bravest most wonderful thing
done by man or by beast, it would just be a sin
if the poor little dog that saved someone's life
lost his instead". Oh, what trouble and strife.

Then someone shouted "what's that over there?"
when limping lazily with pretty grey hair
came a dog with a neckerchief of dark ruby red
and a shock of white hair on top of his head.
He sauntered along looking cool as can be
and glanced at the young boy, then looked up at me.
Because I was there, and so I can say,
I was there the first time this dog saved the day.

3. The Go-Cart Race of '63

The Go-Cart Race of '63
was eagerly awaited.
Now I was just a youngster then
and was really quite elated.
I'd planned for months and built a cart
with pedals to make it go.
I'd trained all through the winter weeks
in wind and rain and snow.

I'd raced before in the previous year
but been run right off the track
by the local bully, a bigger boy,
who we all called 'Lazy Jack' (though only behind his back).

I vowed that year that I would win
the next time that we raced,
for Jack was always beating kids
needed putting in his place.

The day before the race was held
I was practising down my street
when who should appear, but the bully I feared,

with his gang 'The Deadly Elite'.
They pulled me up by my collar and then
Jack knocked me about with his fists,
I fell over and bled and watched as the gang
smashed my go-cart to bits.

They turned and looked at me and said
"Don't race kid, just forget it.
Or we'll finish the job we started today
and make sure you regret it".

I sat feeling wretched, knew not what to do
and just let them all walk away;
a minute went past and there came unasked
a dog who we all thought a stray.

I said "what on earth should I do now?
I really wanted to race,
if I can pluck up the courage to go on and do it,
I'll sure get a smack in the face.
Not only that, I have nothing to ride
and I can't build a cart in a night;
the pedals are bent, the wheels are all buckled,
there's no time to put this thing right".

The dog looked at me with his head to one side
and then he walked up to the cart.
He pulled the four wheels to the side of the road
but this was only the start.
He yanked at the chassis and dragged it to me
and dropped it right at my feet,
it was then we decided (I suppose I mean 'we')
that Jack was going to get beat.

I worked through the night with my helper beside,
I worked as we say 'like a dog'.
I rebuilt the whole cart and good grief it was hard,
I wrestled with steering and cogs.
I mended the wheels, the pedals and seat.
The axle by far the worst bit
but I just got it finished by 7 am,
it was then the fatigue really hit.

Now the race was at 10 from Saint Mary's Church,
I had practically no time to rest,
at half nine I awoke as the dog licked my face,
he was standing up right on my chest.

I leapt up confused and the dog looked bemused
then we both ran out of the door.

I pulled at the car which looked good as new,
Better even perhaps than before.

We lined up at the start and Jack looked annoyed,
drew his finger across his fat neck,
he meant to imply that I was in trouble
but this I had come to expect.

So the gun went off and the race then began,
there were two carts at the front of the pack.
I was pedalling fast and bombing along
keeping up with the Lazy kid Jack.

His cart had a motor, a two-stroke I think,
he was lazy and could not pedal fast,
this meant he was sitting looking smug and he shouted
"I'm gonna make sure that youcome last!".

There were people all watching us racing along
but then when we came to a bend
there was no-one to see us as the pavement ran out,
I was pedalling, so couldn't defend.

Jack leant over with a spanner in his hand
and rammed it straight in my machine,

it got jammed, the cogs seized, the pedals all bent
and slowly I ran out of steam.

I'd stopped in the street, could pedal no more
and Jack laughed as he motored away;
I had no way to move and was sure that I'd lose
but then who turned up? 'Twas the stray.

The little grey dog had a look in his eye
that said "hey kid never give in",
then he grabbed up the rope at the front of the cart
and he looped it round under his chin.

I wasn't quite sure what he meant to do
but then he started to run
and my gosh the cart raced and bounced on the road
the dog, it seemed, having such fun.

We flew past spectators who looked on in awe
and the dog ran incredibly fast.
Lazy Jack smirked as he neared the finish,
it was then that I rocketed past.

We'd won the race! The crowd gave a cheer

for the fastest dog in the land,

I jumped out of the cart with fist in the air

and the Mayor came with trophy in hand.

The crowd grabbed me up, I was carried aloft

when I saw out the edge of my eye

Lazy Jack looking angry was walking toward

the dog who couldn't stand, though he tried.

Jack looked possessed, I could see on his face

he had plans to get his own back,

I screamed "don't you touch him", the crowd stopped to stare

at the shuddering figure of Jack.

Jack thought to himself "they can look I don't care,

I know it's not right and I know it's not fair

I know the dog now is too tired to run,

I'll kick him to death for he ruined my fun,

I'll punch him and throw him, I'll drown him and then,

I'll kick him and slap him and punch him again".

As Jack neared the dog, he raised up his foot,

I leapt in between them and shouted

"If you touch this dog you cowardly lout

I'll make you pay, don't you doubt it"

Now the dog still lay panting, I glanced down at his face,
then I turned and looked up at Jack
who swung his great fist which crashed into my face
with a terrible thunderous crack.
As Jack stood there laughing the dog jumped to his feet
but before he could tackle the thug
the crowd charged the boy and whisked him away
and a girl gave the brave dog a hug.

So the dog was a hero and that day so was I;
sometimes you walk into a smack
and sometimes a stranger might help save your life
and sometimes you'll help save theirs back.
The crowd was still raucous and the girl held the dog
and as she hugged Colin, I carried her,
now I love that dog with all of my heart and as for that girl…. well I
married her.

4. The Busker, The Dog and The Beady Eyed Man

'Twas a bright sunny day
and the air was fair crisp
but you wouldn't have said it was cold;
there was not too much wind,
an unusual thing,
so Katie was feeling quite bold.

For she was a 'busker'
and played a guitar,
with a strum that could make a man weep,
her voice held such tenderness,
was youthful and light
and sometimes was solemn and deep.

She could sing you to beauty
or sing you to fear,
she could inspire like a great work of art;
she could help kids stop crying
and comfort the dying
but best of all fill up your heart.

This day she stopped
by Memorial Hall
and looked for a spot in the sun;
she started by playing
'The Maid of the River'
and then she played 'Your Lonely Gun'.

She'd been playing for hours
and her fingers all stung
and she hardly had noticed the fog
which descended around her
and made her feel cold,
it was then that she noticed the dog.

Just a little way yonder
with head to one side
was a terrier with handsome grey coat;
he had a red scarf
which was tied with a knot
and hung loose around his grey throat.

Then along came a man
with old sunken cheeks
who had greasy black hair on his head;

his eyes were quite beady,

he looked pretty seedy, his pallor had him looking half dead.

He heard the sweet music

and stopped in his tracks

and he looked a little bemused

then he felt something shift

just under his ribs

and this left him rather confused.

It's a magical thing

to hear Katie sing,

what she sang that day moved him inside;

she melted the ice

that had frozen his heart

and then the man started to cry.

She finished the song

and put down her guitar

and she asked the old man what was wrong.

He said he was sad

'cos the whole world was bad,

that he wanted to learn to write songs.

Tho' the man seemed much better

he was still bad inside,

and you know why he was feeling so sad?

Cos he'd lied and he'd cheated,

he'd robbed and he'd fought

and he'd ruined the things that he had.

So he grabbed Katie's money

and the guitar he took too

and he pushed her down onto the floor;

he laughed as he ran

with his new toy in tow

and he headed on up to the moor.

But lest we forget,

Katie's audience was not one,

there was another fan there in the crowd,

the little grey dog

that was watching the scene

looked impressive and angry and proud.

This dog was a legend

known all over the Peaks;

his fame had now travelled wide,

his name was just Colin

but people all loved him and this was what gave Colin pride.

He tore after the thief

and with one fell leap

he had bitten him hard on the leg,

the man turned and screamed

and pulled out a large knife

but Colin was shaking his head.

The man brandished the knife

and swiped at the dog

but Colin leapt out of the way,

The thief lunged at thin air

and so lost his feet

and of course Colin didn't delay.

He jumped at the thug

and pushed him right back

and the man fell down to the floor;

His head hit the curb

He was out for the count,

He twitched once and then moved no more.

Katie still sat on the ground where she fell,

Was crying and shaking with fear;

Colin ran up, put a paw on her hand

then he jumped up and licked Katie's ear.

She giggled and smiled,

she felt better inside

and she picked up her battered guitar,

then she wrote a new song

and it's still going on

about Colin the Wandering Star.

For Colin will be there for all boys and girls

he never will fail to deliver,

he'll be there for anyone needing some help

for Colin will be here forever.

And Colin is there if you ever need him

he'll help if your heart isn't dark,

so help people too whenever you can

and one day you might hear his bark.

5. Dog on the Tracks

On a sunny bright day in the middle of spring
a woman was walking along,
she was getting a train to see her old friend
but was worried she'd get the wrong one.

With her eyes on the board that displayed the times
explaining where each train was going
And her handbag open for the platform to see
she was asking for trouble, not knowing.

Now a naughty young boy saw her purse sticking out
and didn't wait to snap up the prize,
he grabbed the fat purse from the open bag
and ran off in front of her eyes.

When out of nowhere from behind a bench
ran a pretty grey dog toward the boy
but the youngster ran fast straight into the dog
hadn't seen him, so couldn't avoid.

The dog leapt at the boy who fell head over feet
and the purse then flew from his hand;

the dog jumped up quickly and grabbed up the loot

which was all that the dog had then planned.

But the boy found his feet and decided to run

when the station guard shot from his hut

the boy jumped from the platform and onto the tracks,

he thought that he'd be okay but....

Oh help! A train was flying along,

was going to crush the young lad;

the dog saw this coming and then started running,

he knew the boy wasn't so bad.

With seconds to spare the dog leapt on the track

and the boy then looked up in fright

the dog collided with the lad and pushed him hard

and they both flew away out of sight.

The train whipped past in a huff and a puff

of thick dark sooty grey steam

it cleared ever so slowly as your eyes sometimes do

when you wake from a frightening dream.

Now onlookers ran up to the platforms edge

of course, expecting the worst

but there was the boy sat confused but unscathed
then suddenly out the tears burst.

A little way further up the platforms edge
was a little grey dog looking proud;
he wore a little red scarf round his little grey neck,
he would ride on the trains when allowed.

Now he turned and jumped up, up onto the bench
from there leapt on the paper boy's booth
then off he skipped deftly and scrambled aloft
and was stood tall - up high on the roof.

So when the train heading north arrived two minutes later
then secretly the dog could alight,
he would sit on the roof of the train you see
and travel in the evening light.

As the train wound its way through the peaks and the dales
he watched the sun turn red above,
he remembered his life with the circus and friends
and how he had once been in love.

6. Weeping Willow

On a warm sunny day

on a mid-March morn

while the Don wound its way to the sea,

there was a willow tree weeping

and a baby chick yawning

who was sat in a nest in the tree.

His mother off hunting

for worms and for grubs

with which to feed the young chick,

it had been a cold winter

and Daddy Bird, well,

he had been terribly sick.

Daddy Bird had been taken away

to visit the old healing crows,

so mother was struggling

to keep the chick fed

and the chick was just feathers and bones.

On this morning there was

prowling near the river

a large and aggressive old cat;

he was a fat ginger Tom

and as has he sauntered along

he would play with his green felted hat.

He spied in the tree

the nest and the chick

so he jumped to the bottom-most branch,

the willow was thin

and his weight made it wobble

and the chick could not help but to blanch.

At the sight of the cat

the bird chirped in fright

and thought "goodness me what to do?"

I want just to cry

but needs must I fly

it might not be nice but it's true.

So he jumped to the edge

of the twiggerty nest

and readied to take off in flight,

the cat saw this happen

and leapt at the chick

who took off, his knuckles clenched tight.

He drifted for a moment

but soon his wings ruffled

and he started to fall to the floor;

the cat laughed and chuckled

and watched the bird fall

then he leapt from the tree once more.

The bird lay bedraggled

down by the river

and the cat wandered over to watch;

Tom thought "this is easy

I'll have me some lunch,

dining on chick is top notch".

He was ready to pounce

but from far up above

swooped Mother Bird with claws sticking out,

she banged into the cat

who yelped and miaowed

and was muddled and fell all about.

Mother Bird grabbed chick

and put her on a log

that was floating at the edge of the river,

then she turned and made ready

to fight off the cat

who, so angry, had started to quiver.

But gosh, what is this?

The log has now moved,

it's floating away down the stream,

this is too much to bear

Mother Bird cannot see!

This is just like a terrible dream.

So the cat will soon kill

this poor Mother Bird

and the skinny chick surely will drown

and dear Daddy Bird

has been taken away

and the bird's nest has now fallen down.

Blimey!

Then out of the blue

in a flash of grey fur

with a go-faster stripe of bright red,

came a beautiful dog

with a silvery beard

and a shock of white hair on his head.

He jumped on the head
of the big ginger cat
and leapt up high in the air,
the cat fell with a crash
Colin dropped with a splash
by the chick, who grabbed his grey hair.

The chick hopped on his back with a happy little chirp
and the dog doggy-paddled to shore.
The ginger cat ran, for he knew dog had won
and Mother Bird chirped all the more.

The two birds reunited, shed happy fat tears
while Colin just panted and dripped,
Mummy Bird was delighted and thanked the grey dog
and the chick just giggled and skipped.

Our dog said "no problem,
that's just how I roll,
my name is Colin Fontana,
I don't like bad cats
in silly green hats,
and I still wear my sweetheart's bandana".

"Now before I set off
there's one more thing to do,
as you lost your old nest to that cat",
he jumped into the bushes
and came out waving
the ginger Tom's green felted hat.

"Now that's toasty and warm
and will sit in the tree
it's green as well, just like the leaves,
so you'll be quite safe
and not lose your eggs
to magpies and squirrels and thieves".

So Colin turned now,
left the pair to themselves,
ran off with his tail in the air,
then behind he heard laughing
and looked back to see
Daddy Bird standing tall with the pair.

7. Red Neckerchief

I once knew a handsome grey terrier

Who as he got older got merrier

Had a red neckerchief

That could fend off his grief

For his love though he never could bury her

8. The Wolf in the Woods

On a cold winter's night on the way to Forge Dam
was a man in a jacket and scarf,
he was walking along with the wind in his eyes
so he couldn't quite make out the path.

He didn't see coming from the dark of the woods
a wolf with matted black fur
who jumped at the man and ripped out his neck
then he gobbled him up in a blur.

The man was no loss, for his heart wasn't kind
but he's not the cause for this verse,
for the wolf was still hungry and ready to fight
for wolves will just eat 'til they burst.

Now up near the dam on this cold windy night
was a man with his ten year old son.
Though they knew the weather was not looking good
they thought that to camp would be fun.

But they didn't know that they weren't alone
for they weren't aware of the beast

with matted black fur and sharp jagged teeth
that was hunting nearby for a feast.

They sat playing cards and eating some food,
the food maybe gave them away,
when they heard near the tent a terrible noise
that made the man's face ashen grey.

A howl of such pity, a mournful lament
but still angry and stuffed full of hate;
it ripped at the canvas, the boy cried in fear
and the father so shocked dropped his plate.

Now the father could see from the light of the moon
the wolf as he circled the tent,
so he readied himself to defend his young boy,
grabbed a knife, then outside he went.

The wolf bared his teeth and seemed almost to smile
at the frightened small man in the rain,
but he looked past the man and into the tent
and then a thought shot through his brain.

"I spy a young boy, a delectable treat
for the young are more tasty with much younger meat".

Now the man wasn't tough though he had a good heart
he threw himself straight at his foe.
He stabbed with the knife and he cut the wolf's leg
but the man was just simply too slow.

The wolf leapt to one side and reared up on his legs,
sunk his teeth in the shoulder so deep
that the poor man's bone broke and he fell to his knees
and the young boy started to weep.

The wolf turned around and grinning a grin
he licked at his now bloody mouth,
he saw the tent flap blowing free in the wind
and he readied to pull the boy out.
Just then a cloud moved that had covered the moon
and the light that shone down was white blue
and it bounced off a creature that shone like a jewel
that was running just now into view.

"It looks like a dog" the boy had only just thought
when it hit the wolf right in the side
and the wolf fell down yelping and rolling about
and the small silver dog gave a cry.
He howled at the moon and the little boy laughed

for the dog wore a red neckerchief
"I know you, you're Colin, the purge of all foes"
and he sank down with a sigh of relief.

The wolf got to his feet and turned himself round
and he looked at the small silver dog
and he thought "I can kill him with one snap of my jaw
and toss him away to the fog".
This thought made him happy and he turned up his head
and howled a deep deafening note,
at which Colin leapt up and with terrible ease
he ripped out the wolf's bloody throat.

The man by this time had crawled back to the tent
and his son helped him pour a stiff drink
which he knocked back in one to steady his nerves
and helped him come back from the brink.
They looked out of the tent which was still open wide
and saw Colin go walking away;
wondered why he was there and how he had known
he'd be needed to help save the day.

But Colin the dog is just homeless you see
so wanders around on his own;
though he hasn't a bed or a kennel to use

he's used now to living alone.

Thank God for Colin, the best dog of all,

the guardian that walks in the dark.

Though he kills if ever he needs to kill, he lives thinking just with his

heart.

9. The Day the Dog Played Dead

The train flew along and smoke billowed out
as it wove its way through the hills.
This train was unusual and carried the circus
of the Most Magnificent McGill.

It rattled along from town to town
and the villages all between,
it showed the most wondrous and magical things
that man has ever yet seen.

It had lions and tigers, an elephant too
and a seal that balanced a ball,
a trapeze artiste who could fly through mid-air
and a clown who was saddest of all.

There was a bearded lady and one with tattoos
that stretched from her toes to her head,
but the best show of all, if you want my advice,
were the dogs that had learned to play dead.

These dogs were a couple, one girl and one boy;
the boy had a silver-grey coat.

The girl had glossy black fur and bright eyes

and a pretty red scarf round her throat.

Just now they were sitting on the roof of the train,

right there they were sat crossing paws,

looking straight forward with wind in their hair

this life was the good life for sure.

The next day was a big one, they were performing their act

in Endcliffe Park for the King,

for the news of this circus, the Magnificent McGill

had spread from here to Beijing.

The circus would play for the country's elite,

they'd be playing for the highest of praise

but a storm was then brewing, though nobody knew it

a tragedy coming their way.

The dogs awoke early on a bright sunny day,

the men had the tents to put up;

the dogs ran to help whenever they could,

they were the cheeriest and happiest of pups.

They went off to practise with old Grandpa Jo

the fastest shot in the west;

he was 106 and losing the thread
but still he had never yet missed.

So later that day the show went ahead
with the King and his court in the crowd;
the stunts had been grand, the lions were fierce
and the cannon was terribly loud.

The King thought it perfect, the princesses cheered,
the trapeze a massive success;
the clowns were delightful, especially 'Butch'
who was wearing a fine sequin dress.

Fast was approaching the 'Dead Dog' display
and the dogs were just ready to go,
but the problem was someone not there to be seen!
Where on earth is Old Grandpa Jo?

They ran off to find him, they did in no time,
he was sleeping with a bottle in hand;
they barked at him loudly and then licked his face
and hastened him quickly to stand.

He looked a bit sozzled but rushed to his tent,
he stumbled and struggled to run,

he got to the door and staggered inside,

he bent down and picked up a gun.

But this gun was different and didn't hold blanks

but Jo didn't see the mistake,

so off the three ran, to the world's biggest top

but this time the deaths won't be fake.

Just like in rehearsal the dogs forward roll

and the King and the courtiers cheer,

when they walked on their hind legs everyone laughed

but we're coming to the end that we fear.

Old Grandpa Jo walked out to the dogs

not acting but really quite stoned,

the crowd all went silent as he pulled out the gun,

then the audience nervously groaned.

Jo then said, acting "you dogs are too rude,

and you're constantly messing about,

I'll teach you, I'll learn you, I'll show you, I will

I'm going to blow both your lights out"

Bang

Bang

Now at once poor Jo knew something was wrong
and a silence then fell like a veil,
when he saw the blood flow from the dogs that he loved
he collapsed and went deathly pale.

He clutched at his chest and let out a sigh
and then he fell back and he died,
he had broken his heart cos he'd killed his own friends
and his soul drifted into the sky.

Now the dogs were just lying, quiet and still
for they'd both been shot by the gun;
but wait, boy dog's moving, he's started to twitch,
he's getting up! How is this done?

So Old Grandpa Jo was the best shot of all,
he'd never missed ever before
but the cruellest of twists this time he had missed
but just once, 'cos girl dog's no more.

The dog's name was Colin, he looked at his friend
who lay like she slept on the floor,
then he howled at the world and his little heart broke
and he felt like he'd never before.

Now the circus was over. This was the end.

The King was shocked and appalled.

It was a disaster that shook this whole fair isle,

circus gone, once and for all.

Poor Colin sat still and looked at his friend

for 101 days and nights;

when anyone came to move them away

he'd bark and snarl and bite.

The circus left town, the seasons passed on,

Colin sat with a dead weight inside;

there was lead in his heart, no fire in his chest

and his wet eyes would sting while he cried.

...

Now 101 days is a very long time

to sit still and wait with your love,

to go without food and water and bed,

most anyone would have given up.

But this dog isn't normal and mourned he had long

101 days in respect,

then he got up and barked and untied her scarf
and tied it up tight round his neck.

From that day forward Colin remained
as faithful as ever he should
to the memory of his partner, his soul mate, his love
for their life had been a life that was good.

So now he's a Wonder Dog with a heart that is whole
and his love for his girl still endures
and nothing can stop him as he travels around
for his intentions are honest and pure.

10. 101 Days and Nights

The little dog ran
along the path
with his tail stuck high in the air,
there were tears in his eyes
and ice in his heart
and blood in his shaggy grey hair.

There were trees either side
that waved and moaned
and they leaned right over the path
and a cold rattlin' wind
whipped up through the leaves
and they whispered a sinister laugh.

Then a cloud moved aside
the moon gave a wink
and a shadow appeared on the ground,
just metres ahead
with a drink in his hand
a leering and jeering old clown.

The little dog stopped,

he was scared of the clown,

he turned with his tail 'tween his legs;

the clown tipped his drink

and opened up wide

and sucked out the last of the dregs.

The dog tried to run

but he just couldn't move

then he felt a rumbling roar.

A screaming began,

a crack then appeared

and the dog fell straight through the floor.

There was nothing beneath

but he soon heard a sound,

a squawking way off to the right

he was falling and twisting

and all was pitch dark

as he fell through the inkiest night.

The moon was beneath him

it looked mournful and sad

and it frowned as the little dog fell

the little dog laughed

to see such fun

and the fear in his doggy heart swelled.

He fell at the moon

for minutes or more

but when he was finally to crash

he saw ripples and waves,

'twas water you see

and he plunged in with a terrible smash.

Now he opened is eyes

as cold water pressed down,

he drifted for night after night;

he breathed not at all

he had nothing to eat

and saw nothing, no darkness or light.

Then the small dog felt sand

on his wrinkled wet paws

he felt warmth on his soggy grey back;

he blinked open his eyes

and winced with surprise

for the world was no longer black.

He walked on a beach

at the edge of the sea

with the warmth of the sun washing in,

the grief now had passed

and left him complete

with a shock of white hair on his chin.

The dog ran in circles

and rolled in the waves

and barked as he thought of his friend.

I'm ready to go back

my sadness is gone

I'm ready to have fun again.

Epilogue: The Story Continues

So Colin the dog is a lot older now,

He lives in the woods by a stream.

His tale hasn't ended. Just like you and I,

He's part of a much bigger scheme.

This world is a wonder, so don't miss a trick,

never worry about tears you have cried.

Throw yourself at adventure and fight the good fight

and at least if you fail you'll have tried!

Here's to Colin!

Printed in Great Britain
by Amazon